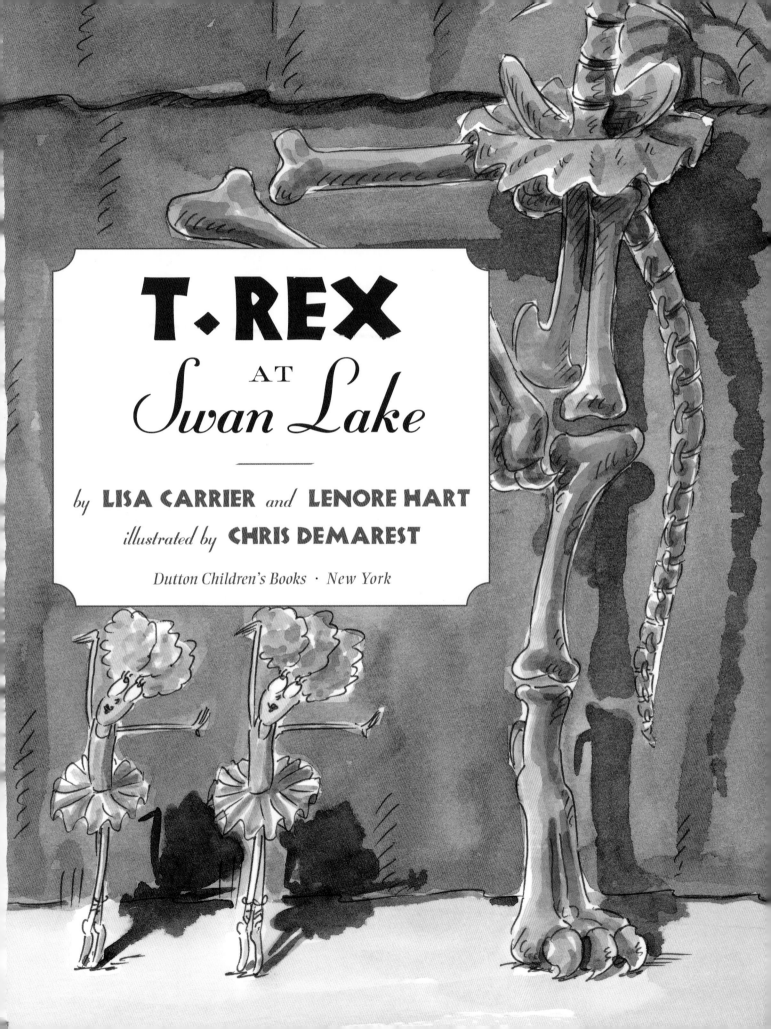

T·REX
AT
Swan Lake

by **LISA CARRIER** *and* **LENORE HART**
illustrated by **CHRIS DEMAREST**

Dutton Children's Books · New York

Published in the United States by Dutton Children's Books,
a division of Penguin Young Readers Group
345 Hudson Street, New York, New York 10014
www.penguin.com

Designed by Tim Hall · Manufactured in China
ISBN 0-525-47177-4
First Edition
1 3 5 7 9 10 8 6 4 2

To my mom and Dr. Seuss
L.C.

For Kay Hart and Naia Poyer,
two as strong and determined as T. Rex!
L.H.

For Trish—make no bones about it
C.D.

T. REX was bored. For ninety-nine years, not much had changed in the Dinosaur Hall at the Natural History Museum.

Usually she enjoyed being the center of attention. People stared at her and gasped.

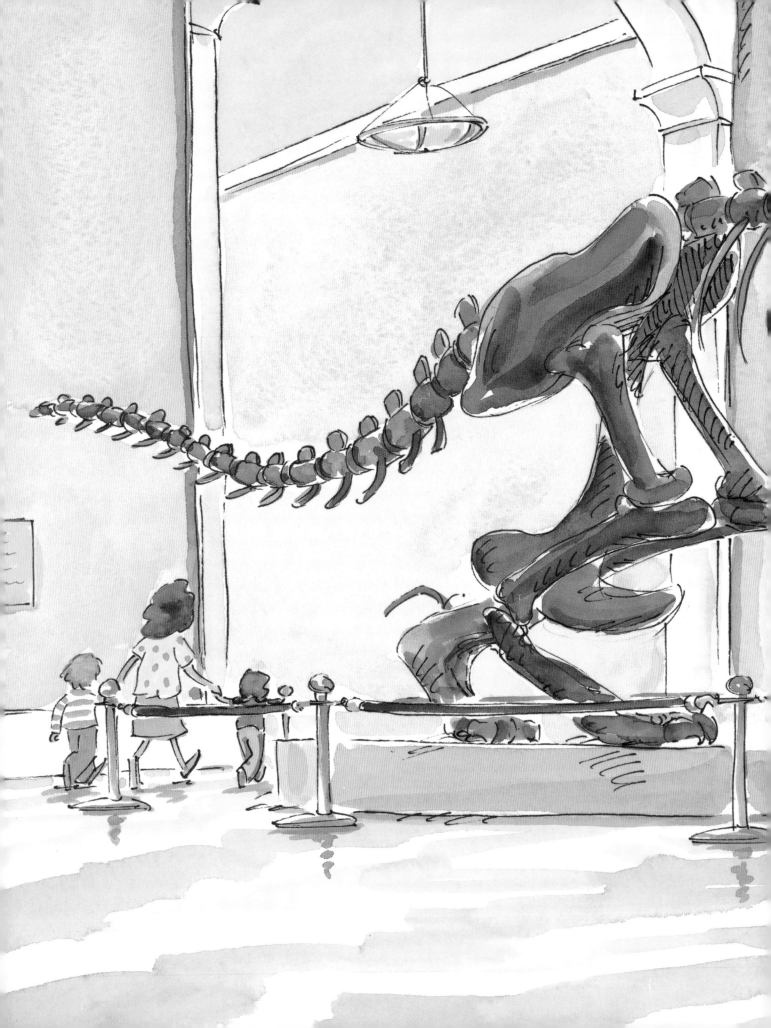

She even had her own guard, who stood proudly at attention, keeping people from getting too close. Sometimes, when no one else was around, he told her about his day. T. Rex always listened politely.

T. Rex knew she impressed museum visitors. But being a star wasn't always enough. She missed the old days, millions of years ago, when she ran free. It had been a happy time of leaping in green meadows and tiptoeing through clear streams, bending to drink the fresh, cool water. Remembering the old life made it difficult for her to enjoy the admiring crowds.

One afternoon, two ladies came into the hall and stopped in front of her. They were talking about something they called "the ballet." T. Rex tilted her head to listen.

"*Swan Lake* is on tonight. Two blocks down, at the Opera House. It's my absolute favorite," said the woman in green. "I love to watch the ballerinas twirl and spring across the stage! The Swan Princess leads them like this." The green woman stood on tiptoe.

T. Rex tried to rise up on her toes, too. But she'd forgotten that her feet were bolted to the floor.

"Of course there's a handsome prince," the woman added. "But that nasty villain makes me shiver!"

No problem, thought T. Rex. I could take care of him with one bite.

Ballet sounds exactly like what I've been missing all these years. I've got to try it, T. Rex decided. Right now!

There was the small problem of her bolted-down toes. But she flexed her powerful knees, and with two great yanks pulled her aching feet loose from the platform.

Goodness, that was easy, she thought, and lumbered toward the exit. Crowds of shouting visitors scattered like flocks of noisy, prehistoric chickens.

"Stop!" called her guard. "You can't leave!"

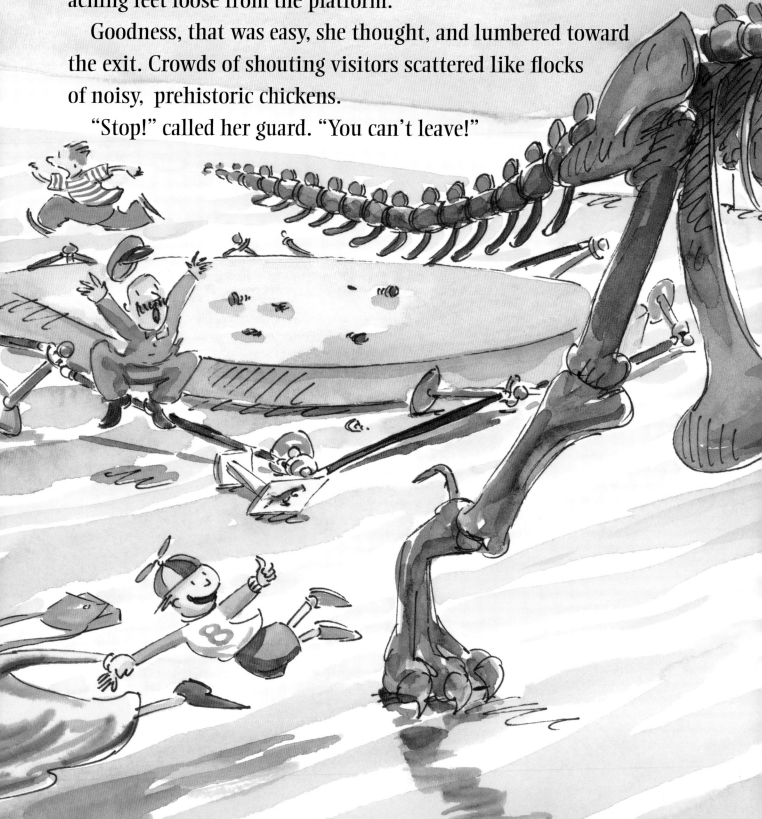

Outside, T. Rex paused for a moment, dazzled by her first glimpse of sunlight in ninety-nine years. She took in a deep breath of fresh air and then clattered down the road.

But on the street there was more screaming and yelling. "Stop!" shouted a police officer, waving his arms. "You can't be out here!"

"Oh, but I am," T. Rex said, holding up one of her newly freed feet. "Isn't it wonderful?"

It was nothing like the old days, though. The ground was teeming with people of all shapes and sizes, running in all directions.

I hope it will be more peaceful at the Opera House,
T. Rex thought.

She squeezed through the back door of the Opera House.
It *was* more peaceful here. Dark, cool, quiet as a cave.
Where are all the people? T. Rex wondered. She climbed the backstage ladder to get a better view. She carefully tiptoed along the cat-
walk. The only sound was her joints clickety-clacking against the
metal rungs. She ducked under snarls and loops of cables that
reminded her of lovely hanging vines from her past.

Since the other ballerinas hadn't arrived yet, she decided to curl up for a little nap. She dreamed of the old days.

Then T. Rex heard the faint sounds of music. She lifted her head. The orchestra was tuning up. On the stage, dancers posed and stretched. Stagehands rushed about, putting scenery in place. T. Rex's eye sockets grew wide with astonishment. "It's even better than I'd imagined!" She clapped her claws as ballerinas swirled like fish caught in a current. Spectacular! Tremendous! It made her very hungry.

T. Rex was so enthralled she nearly forgot she had come to dance. But the ballerinas were all so fancy, and she looked so plain. She needed a costume, too.

When T. Rex squeezed into the wardrobe room, the costume mistress took one look and fainted dead away. So T. Rex had to help herself. But all of the costumes were so tiny! She finally managed to squeeze her hipbones into an extra-large, stretchy tutu. No problem, she decided. I'll just hold my breath until the show's over!

Once she was dressed, she couldn't wait. In her old life, she'd always enjoyed making a dramatic entrance. So she vaulted up the backstage ladder in four big steps, grabbed one of the hanging vines, and swooped like a falling pterodactyl down to the stage.

Unfortunately, she overshot a bit.

"Oops," cried T. Rex as she slammed into a man waving a stick.

It was the conductor. "Oh, dear. So sorry."

The music stopped. The Opera House was silent.

"No, no. This won't do," T. Rex scolded. "The show must go on."
She picked up the conductor's baton and waved it as he had done.
The clarinet player gasped. A violinist ran away screaming. The
other musicians all looked very nervous, but at last they started
playing again.

T. Rex gently lifted the conductor back onto his podium. "I'm sorry. Terribly clumsy of me." She smiled apologetically. "Love your outfit."

The trembling conductor stared at her teeth. He gulped as T. Rex handed him his baton. "Thank you," he squeaked.

"Oh, it was nothing," she said modestly. "Keep up the good work!"

Now for my debut, T. Rex decided. Let's start with some easy spins and a twirl or two. She raised her arms, rose up on her toes, and then . . .

She turned and leaped and whirled, pretending she was back in the meadow, the cool breeze in her face, the soft grass beneath her claws. She whipped her tail joyfully.

She didn't really mean to knock anyone off the stage.
"Oh dear, so sorry!" she called over her shoulder.

Then she saw a man in white tights watching from the wings. Ah, the prince, she thought, and spun even faster to impress him. But as she finished her final pirouette, T. Rex noticed that another man had come onto the stage.

Hmm, she thought, this must be the bad guy. What had the lady in green called him? Oh, yes—the villain.

She didn't much care for the way he was scowling at her, as if she didn't belong.

So she did what came naturally.
And it felt good.

The other ballerinas shrieked and ran away,
their fluffy tutus flapping gracefully.

Then T. Rex performed thirty-two perfect pirouettes, sixteen dainty cat steps, and one tremendous leap across the stage. For her grand finale, she balanced on one toe-claw, her knee joints clattering like pebbles in a blender.

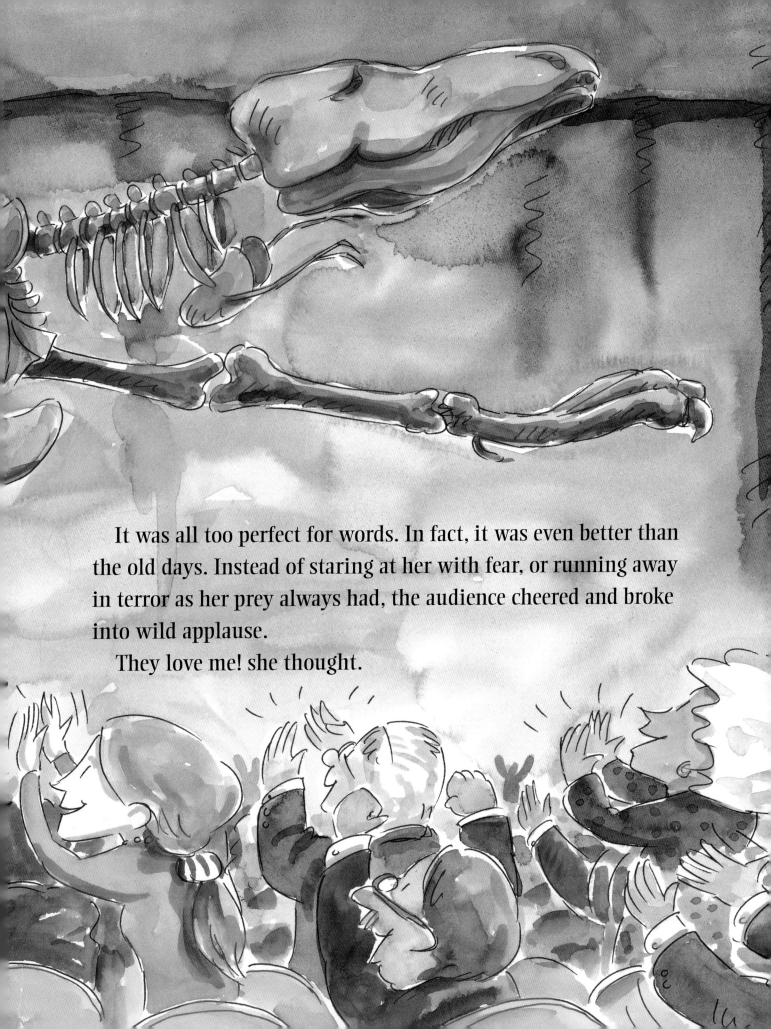

It was all too perfect for words. In fact, it was even better than the old days. Instead of staring at her with fear, or running away in terror as her prey always had, the audience cheered and broke into wild applause.

They love me! she thought.

Satisfied at last, T. Rex fell back into the arms of her partner. But it wasn't the prince. He had fainted in the wings. She saw that her partner was her very own guard from the museum. "I was so worried!" said her guard as he gently helped her up. "I've been looking for you everywhere!"

T. Rex was so glad to see him. More than anyone else, she had wanted him to watch her wonderful dance.

After a standing ovation, five curtain calls, and three dozen roses, the guard said it was time to go. T. Rex didn't mind. It had been a very tiring evening. So he escorted her back to her spot at the museum.

There she stands to this day, admired by many visitors. And on long afternoons, she and her guard talk about her wonderful ballet debut.

And every night, after all the people have gone home and the museum doors are locked, she remembers that great performance. T. Rex is sure that one day she will return to the stage. After all, Christmas is coming, and she knows what that means . . .

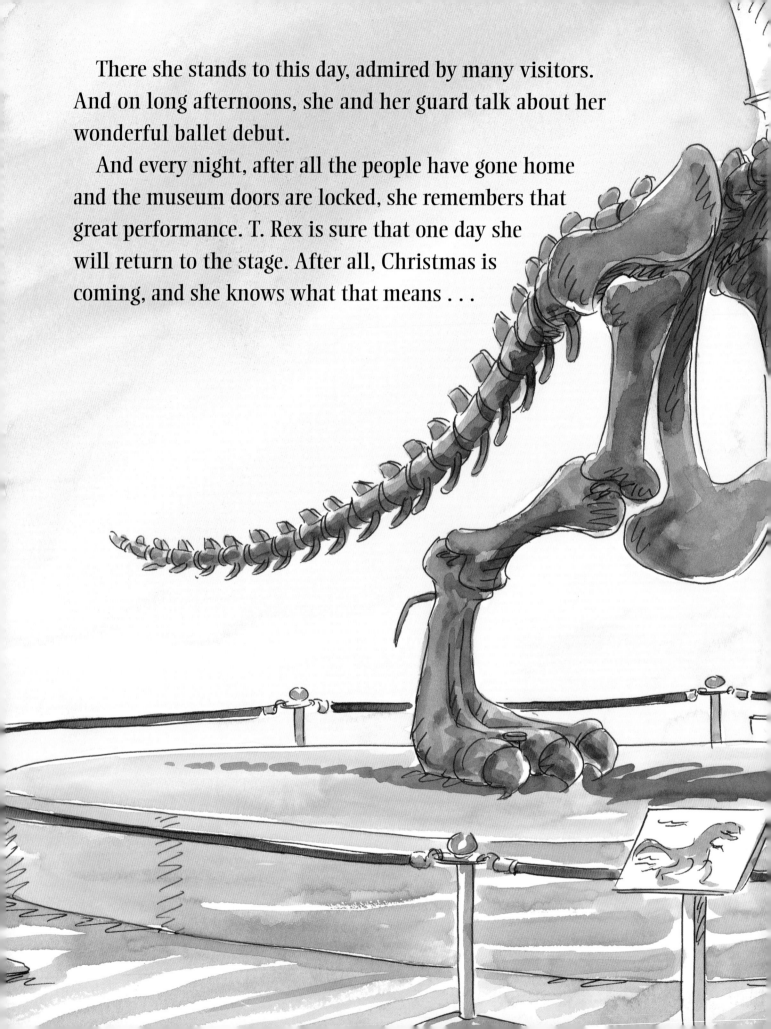

. . . the annual performance of *The Nutcracker*. T. Rex knows she'd be perfect as the Sugar Plum Fairy.